A Great Idea?

By Anastasia Suen
Illustrated by Jane Dippold

TABLE OF CONTENTS

Chapter 1: Waiting to Ride 4
Chapter 2: Choosing a Trail 11
Chapter 3: Let's Ride! 18
Chapter 4: Something Blue 25
Chapter 5: Don't Get Caught
　　　　　Holding the Bag 32
Chapter 6: Your Secret's Safe
　　　　　With Me 40
Ending 1: Out of the Bag 51
Ending 2: Stop and Breathe 63
Ending 3: Ask for Help 71
Write Your Own Ending 80

CHAPTER 1

Waiting to Ride

Last period. Science. My teacher, Mr. Franks, was standing up at the front of the class. "We'll take the last part of the period to review for the test."

I started drawing bicycles in my notebook. I had been riding my bike after school since I was in kindergarten. As soon as I got home, I ate a snack and then rode my bike until dinnertime. I could ride my bike every day as long as I followed the safety rule: always ride with a partner.

When I started fifth grade, Mom gave me a cell phone. "I want you to keep this in your pocket at all times, Andy," she said.

"Thanks," I said, and then I put the phone in my pocket right away.

"Turn it on first, Andy," Mom said, laughing.

"Oh, right," I said, rolling my eyes.

My friend Josh had laughed, too. His mom worked in an office on the other side of town, so he had gotten his own cell phone in third grade. A new phone was no big deal to him, but to me, well, it was a big deal.

I turned on the phone and the screen lit up.

"I can help you set up your contacts," said Josh.

"Awesome," I said.

"Now that you're in fifth grade, you can ride without an adult," Mom said. Then she pointed at Josh. "You know the rule."

Josh smiled. "Always ride with a partner," he said.

Josh lived across the street from me. I had known Josh ever since I could remember. He was in fifth grade, just like me.

I wasn't allowed to ride my bike alone, not in the hills behind my house anyway. On the street in front of the house, oh, that was fine. I went round and round the cul-de-sac.

Josh and I even had a ramp. It was fun to ride up the ramp and jump into the air. After we landed, we circled back and did it again. And again and again and again.

The ramp was fun, but riding in the hills behind our house was so much better. It wasn't the same thing over and over. Every jump was different, and after you did the jump, you didn't have to go back and do it all over again. You just kept riding to the next one and the next one.

"Andy," said a voice. "Care to join us?" It was Mr. Franks.

I looked up, and the whole class was staring at me. Even Josh. I didn't want to get in trouble. Not now! It wasn't windy and it wasn't rainy. It was a perfect day to ride.

"I'm sorry, can you repeat the question?" I said, looking at the teacher politely.

Mr. Franks already knew I wasn't paying attention. I better be polite and apologize. No need to get detention or extra homework because I was thinking about riding my bike.

Mr. Franks nodded. "As I was saying, are all snakes hatched from eggs?"

Oh! I knew the answer to that one. "No, some snakes are born live."

"Good," said Mr. Franks, and then he looked away. *Whew!* No detention or extra homework for me today. Josh gave me a thumbs-up.

But then Mr. Franks noticed Josh and his thumb. Uh-oh! Josh liked to talk. Oh, did he ever. But he didn't always get his facts straight, and when you pointed that out, he didn't want to budge.

"So you like that," said Mr. Franks. "Here's a question for you. Which snake is larger, the male or the female?"

"Oh, everyone knows males are bigger than females," said Josh.

Emma gave Josh a funny look, but she didn't say anything. It was Megan, Miss Know-It-All, who did that.

Before Mr. Franks could say a word, Megan said in a loud voice, "No, that's not right. The female snakes are larger."

Mr. Franks nodded. "Thank you, Megan. Yes, that is correct."

"But what about your old snake, Mr. Franks?" stammered Josh. "Cornflower was big."

Megan and her friends started laughing. Josh's face began to turn red. Emma rolled her eyes and shook her head. She lived two streets away from us, so she knew how Josh could get. Josh was wrong, dead wrong, again, but he wasn't going to let it go. He just had to be right, no matter what, even when he was wrong.

Mr. Franks walked over to the empty terrarium on the shelf at the back of the classroom. Cornflower had lived in that terrarium until he died at the beginning of the school year. "Yes, Cornflower was big, but that was because he lived so long. Snakes continue to grow their entire lives."

Mr. Franks touched the glass at the top of the terrarium. "I had him for almost ten years before he died," he said in a soft voice.

Ring!

The bell! School was over, thank goodness. I picked up my science book, my notebook, and my pencil. Good-bye school, hello bike ride.

Chapter 2

Choosing a Trail

I ran out the classroom door and down the hallway to the coat hook with my backpack on it. I shoved my books, notebooks, and pencils inside. My backpack was full to the top now that everything was in it. After I got home I would dump everything out and add a water bottle and a snack for my ride.

Josh's coat hook was on the other side of the hallway. It was just like our houses. His house was on one side of the street and mine was on the other.

I put on my backpack and walked over. "Where do you want to ride bikes after school?"

"We rode the Dog Walker's Trail yesterday, so let's go somewhere else," said Josh as we walked down the hallway. It was jammed with kids making their getaway from school.

We reached the middle of the hallway and there was Miss Know-It-All Megan talking with her friends.

Megan smiled at Josh. "Hey, Josh," she said.

"Hey," said Josh, and the girls standing around Megan giggled.

"What's that about?" I asked as we walked away.

Josh shrugged. "Who knows?"

"Girls!" I said and then changed the subject. "What about the Ridge Trail?" It was up on the ridge of the hills so it felt like you were riding at the top of the world.

We walked out the front door of the school. There were kids and parents everywhere.

"No, not that one," said Josh.

"What about the Hidden Trail?" I said. That trail was hard to see from the road. It was the longest one, so we usually saved it for the weekends. But today was different. "At the bus stop this morning, your mom said she would be home late. That would give us time to ride the whole trail."

Josh turned to dodge a kid riding his bicycle home. "If Mom is going to be late, we can ride over to the rock pit and look for fossils," said Josh.

A trip to the rock pit was too long for a school day, but I didn't say anything. We walked down the sidewalk past a long line of yellow school buses. Our bus was second to last. Our bus driver, Henry, was standing in front of the bus talking to another driver.

Josh and I climbed up the steps into the bus. I liked to sit by the window, so I could look outside. And Josh always wanted to be on the aisle to see everyone, so it was perfect.

"Hey, Jon. Hey, Nick," said Josh. He talked to every fifth grade boy we saw as we walked to the back of the bus. Only the fifth grade boys sat at the back of the bus. The fifth grade girls, like Emma, sat in the front. All of the other kids sat in the middle.

I walked to a row two windows from the back and sat down. Now I could see everything. Josh followed me and sat on the aisle. I looked at the kids by the bike rack. I wished we lived close enough to

ride our bikes, but we had to ride on the highway to get to our houses.

There was one good thing about living so far away. We lived at the end of everything. No more houses. No more roads. At the end of our road, it was all mountains. Not big mountains, mind you, small ones. They were hills, really, and they were perfect for riding bikes.

I turned to face Josh. Maybe if I acted like we were going to ride somewhere else he would forget about the rock pit. "Let's ride the Switchback Trail today."

"No, I want to go out to the rock pit," said Josh.

"On a school day?" I said. "But it takes so long just to get there."

"But my mom is going to be late, remember?" said Josh.

Here we go again. "But we don't have enough time to go out and look," I replied. "Why ride all that way there if we can't look for fossils?"

Josh looked down. "But . . ."

"But it's a school night," I said. "If I'm not back by dinner I get grounded. My mom isn't going to be late. She'll be waiting for us at the bus stop."

"And if I ride without you and my mom finds out . . . ," said Josh.

"Then you will get grounded, too," I said.

"I don't want to get grounded. Not again," said Josh.

"We can take the Flat Top Trail," I said. "When we go out on that trail we always get back in time. Maybe there are some fossils there for you?"

"Maybe," said Josh.

"Well . . . ," I said, and then I waited. Josh liked to think he was in charge, so he had to say where we were going. He had to make the final decision, or he wouldn't do it.

"What if we go to the rock pit on Saturday?" said Josh. "Then we'll have all day to look for fossils."

"We can do that," I said.

"Okay, then let's ride the Flat Top Trail today," said Josh. "Deal?"

"Deal," I said, and we slapped our hands in the air. It was going to be a great day after all.

Chapter 3

Let's Ride!

I looked out the window and saw Mom's car as the bus pulled up to our stop. Josh's mom dropped us off in the morning on her way to work, and my mom picked us up in the afternoon.

Our bus stop was the first stop in the morning and the last stop in the afternoon. There were only nine kids left on the bus. Emma, Josh, and I were the only fifth graders at our stop.

I put on my backpack and followed Josh as we walked down the aisle. "We can ride bikes as soon as we get home."

"After I get something to eat, I'll meet you at the bottom of the hill," said Josh.

I nodded. Yes, that's how we did it every day. It was good-bye school and hello bike ride—almost! I jumped down the bus steps. I had been waiting all day to ride my bike.

"Hello, boys," said Mom after we got in the car. "How was school today?"

"Fine," we both responded. *Why do grown-ups always ask that?*

"I made some chocolate chip cookies for your snack," Mom said.

"Yum!" said Josh.

"Andy will bring some over for you, won't you, Andy?" said Mom.

"Sure," I said. Well, that took care of finding something to eat after school. All I needed to do now was empty out my backpack and fill up my water bottle. We would eat out on the trail, like we always did.

Mom drove onto our street and stopped the car in front of Josh's garage. "Here you are," she said.

"Thanks, Mrs. J," said Josh as he opened the car door.

"You're welcome," Mom said.

"I'll see you in a few minutes," I said.

"I'll be over after I get my bike and my water bottle," said Josh.

Josh closed the door and then Mom backed down the driveway and drove into our garage. There was my bike, just waiting for me to ride it. The helmet was hanging on the handlebars.

"What are your plans for this afternoon?" said Mom as she turned off the car.

"Josh and I are going to ride bikes on Flat Top Trail," I said as I opened the car door.

"Sounds like fun!" said Mom.

I went into my room and dumped everything out of my backpack. Out came the books, notebooks, and pencils. Good-bye school. Now my backpack was empty, and I was almost ready to go out. Hello bike ride.

I ran to the kitchen, filled up my water bottle, and put it in my backpack. Mom handed me two paper bags. "One for you, and one for Josh."

"Thanks," I said and put the bags in my backpack. I zipped it up nice and tight and put it over my shoulders. I was ready to go.

"Phone?" said Mom as I walked toward the door.

I patted my back pocket.

"Keep it on," said Mom. "Just in case."

"Okay," I said. She always sent me a text when it was time to come back. "Dinner" was all it said, but I knew that meant I needed to go home. We didn't start eating dinner until everyone was home.

Mom patted my hair. "Have fun." I smiled.

I went into the garage. I put on my helmet and rode my bike out of the garage. When I got to the end of the driveway, I saw Josh riding his bike down the hill. Flat Top Trail, here we come. It was finally time to ride!

I was the first to reach the big flat rock at the top of the first hill. I was always the one who led the way on our trail rides. Josh liked to "watch our six." That was a saying he learned on TV. It meant to watch your back, to look behind you and see what was happening.

I put my bike down on the middle of the dirt path and took off my helmet. Josh came up behind me and did the same. I took the two bags out of my backpack and gave one to Josh.

"Mmm, it's still warm," said Josh as he took a big bite of his cookie.

"Just the way I like it," I said. We sat on the rock and ate the warm cookies. It was a good day.

"Hey, what is that?" said Josh. He pointed at a bird circling overhead.

"It's just a hawk," I said. Hawks flew around here all the time.

The hawk flew down to the ground and then back up.

"But what does it have in its talons?" said Josh. "What is long and blue all the way out here?" Josh looked at me.

I shrugged my shoulders. I didn't know, and I really didn't care. It was probably just trash. Birds make their nests out of all kinds of things they find on the ground. Why did it matter anyway?

"I have to find out," said Josh as he stood up and brushed his hands together. Crumbs fell onto the rock.

"The answer is down there," he said, and then he started climbing down the other side of the hill.

Chapter 4

Something Blue

"Wait, what about our bike ride?" I stood up and looked down the hill at Josh. But he didn't answer me.

I climbed down to the bottom of the hill after him and looked around, but I didn't see him anywhere. Why did he have to pull a disappearing act on me?

"Josh, where are you?" I yelled.

"Over here!" said Josh, and then I saw him waving his arm by a large sumac bush.

I walked through the tall grass toward the bush. The sooner we solved this mystery, the sooner we could go back and ride.

When I reached him, Josh was bent over looking at a nest of blue snakes—lots and lots of blue snakes. There must have been a dozen of them, all in one place! No wonder the hawk had been circling.

Josh turned and looked me in the eye. "I have a great idea. I'm going to take one home."

I shook my head. "The last time you had a great idea you were grounded for two weeks! Remember the quail eggs?"

"It wasn't my fault a snake ate them," said Josh. "Snakes have to eat, too."

"But your mom said she didn't want any snakes near her house, remember?" I replied.

Josh looked at the snake nest. "Well, what if I bring one to school?"

"Are you crazy?" I said. "You can't bring a snake to school."

"Mr. Franks had a snake at school," said Josh. "Why can't I bring one?"

I hated to admit it, but Josh had a point. Mr. Franks did have a snake at school, well until it died this year. But it had been there ever since we had been in kindergarten.

"That's true," I said. "But what will you do with it?"

"Put it in Megan's desk," said Josh. "I bet she jumps out of her desk and starts screaming." Josh jumped up and threw his hands in the air as he pretended to be Megan. "Aaahhh, it's a snake!!!!"

I couldn't help but laugh.

"Help me take one of the snakes out of the nest," said Josh.

"And how are we going to do that?" I asked. "Just go up and grab it with our hands?"

A few minutes passed as we both watched those little blue snakes crawl all over each other in the dirt. But Josh didn't say anything. "How did the hawk catch the snake?" I asked.

"With his hands, well, his feet," said Josh.

"Well, I am not picking up a snake with my hands or my feet," I said.

"No, I'll do that," said Josh. Like always, he wanted to be the one in charge.

"I don't think that's a good idea," I said. "What if the snake bites you?"

"Oh, it won't bite me," said Josh. "It's just a baby snake."

"But what if it does," I said. "What if the venom gets into your hand and you die from the poison?"

"Well, baby rattlesnakes are very poisonous," said Josh. "But these aren't rattlesnakes."

"How do you know?" I said. "Maybe they're just too young to have rattles."

Josh pointed at the snake nest. "Rattlesnakes aren't blue, and these snakes are. So they must be garter snakes. Garter snakes aren't poisonous. Well, not to humans, anyway. The poison on their tongues only hurts their prey."

"Okay, so they're not poisonous," I said. "But how are you going to pick one up and carry it home? You can't ride a bike if you're holding a snake with both hands."

So how could he carry it? I looked around and then I saw a small stick on the ground. I walked over and picked it up. "How about this?"

Josh took the stick from my hand. "I can hold one end . . ."

"And carry the snake with the other," I said.

"I can't take this stick to school though," said Josh.

I laughed. "No, Henry wouldn't let you on the bus with a stick or a snake."

"And my mom definitely won't let me bring a snake in her car," said Josh.

"No, she would never do that," I agreed.

"But if she doesn't know about it . . . ," said Josh, and he patted his backpack and smiled.

"You're going to put a snake in your backpack," I said. "Are you out of your mind?"

"It will fit. It's only a baby snake," said Josh.

"But won't it get squished by all your books?" I said.

"I'll just carry my books," said Josh.

"You'll carry your books while you're wearing a backpack," I said. "Won't that give it away?"

"How? The snake will be hiding in my backpack," said Josh.

"But someone might ask why you're carrying your books," I said.

"Well," said Josh, "I can carry them in a separate bag."

"A bag . . . ," I said. "That's it! Use the cookie bag to carry the snake home."

"That's a great idea, Andy!" said Josh, slapping me on the back.

Josh took off his backpack and unzipped it. His paper bag was still inside. We always carried out our own trash.

"All right," said Josh as he handed me his paper bag. "We have a plan. I'll pick up the snake with the stick, and you'll hold the bag."

Chapter 5

Don't Get Caught Holding the Bag

Wait, why was I the one holding the bag and putting out my hands by the snake's mouth? I wasn't the one who wanted the snake. Josh was. I just wanted to ride bikes. How did he talk me into these things anyway?

"My water bottle might crush the snake," said Josh. "Can you hold it for me?" He put down the stick and reached into his backpack. This was my chance.

"Sure, give it to me," I said. Then I quick put the bag on the ground and grabbed the stick.

Josh handed me the water bottle. Then he noticed I was holding the stick. "Wait, why do you have the stick? I need you to hold the bag for me while I catch the snake."

"I found the stick," I said. Josh knew the rule, finders, keepers. He said that to me all the time when he didn't want to share something he'd found. "And you're the one who wants the snake, not me. I just wanted to ride bikes, remember?"

"Oh, all right, you don't have to whine," said Josh.

I looked Josh in the eye. "I'm not whining. I'm just stating the facts."

"Okay, okay, I'll hold the bag," said Josh. "But if you can't get the snake, then I get to hold the stick."

"Come on, let's get this over with," I said as I walked closer to the pit. The baby snakes were still crawling all over each other. I put the stick into the middle of the pit so one of them could crawl on it.

But the little blue snakes moved away from the stick. "Come on. Climb up the stick," I whispered. But not one of them did.

"Let me try," said Josh, as he grabbed for the stick.

"The snakes are still wiggling around," I whispered, as I elbowed him out of the way. And then finally, one of the snakes circled the bottom of the stick.

"Now lift the stick," said Josh.

"I *will*, Josh!"

I lifted the stick, but the snake fell off and landed on the other snakes. They wiggled and then they all started moving the other way.

"Do something, Andy!" said Josh.

I put the stick in front of another snake so it could climb up. I held the stick still like it was just a branch on a tree and waited. The little blue snake started to climb up the stick.

"Now swing it over here," said Josh.

I held the stick still as the baby snake slowly wiggled up the stick. "I don't want it to fall off again. Wait until it climbs a little higher."

"It's higher now," said Josh.

"Okay, are you ready?" I asked.

"Ready," said Josh, and he held the paper bag out at arm's length.

"But what if it hits your hand?" I asked.

"Baby snakes don't bite," said Josh.

"Put the bag on the ground," I said. "You can grab it after the snake gets inside."

"Okay, okay," said Josh. He leaned over and put the bag on the ground near the edge of the snake pit.

I lifted the stick slowly and moved it toward the bag. But as I raised the stick, the snake fell off!

"Let me try," said Josh, trying to grab the stick away from me again.

I gave him another elbow jab. "No, let me do it."

"But you're not doing it," said Josh. "Just let me have a turn."

I stopped and looked at Josh. Wait a minute! Getting the snake wasn't *my* idea. Why was I trying to catch it? "Okay," I said, handing Josh the stick. "Show me how it's done."

"About time," he said. He held the stick still as a baby snake slowly wiggled up it. He then lifted it up so the snake hung over the stick like a rope. "Now into the bag," he whispered. Then he pulled the stick out of the bag and folded the edges over.

"Let's go!" said Josh, and he started walking back toward the big flat rock. "I can't wait to put it in

Megan's desk in science class. We'll see what she has to say about snakes then! Ha!"

"But what about Mr. Franks," I said. "Won't he get mad?"

"Then I'll put it in her backpack," said Josh as we walked back to the top of the hill. "I can watch her freak out when she opens the bag at lunch!"

"And get detention for a week," I said.

"Just kidding," said Josh as we reached the top of the hill.

But was he just kidding? I was never quite sure when it came to Josh. Sometimes he talked big and didn't do anything. And other times he got us both into big trouble. I decided to change the subject. "Let's ride to the end of the trail," I said.

"No, I want to go back and find out what to feed our snake," said Josh.

"*Your* snake," I said. Having a pet snake wasn't my idea of fun. You had to take care of pets and do things like feed them and clean up after them. I didn't want to do all of that work when the snake would do it for itself if I just left it outside.

"Yeah, fine, my snake," said Josh.

"Let me go first," said Josh as he put on his bike helmet. "You can watch my six and see if the snake gets out of the backpack."

"How is it supposed to do that?"

"I don't know," said Josh. "But what if it does? Just let me know."

"Just zip it tight," I said, and then I took off down the trail as

fast as I could. It was all downhill from here, just like my afternoon. Then I felt my phone vibrate. It was time for dinner already. Great. Just great. The whole afternoon was lost. I only got to ride up one hill and back down again because of that snake. And Josh's "great" idea. What a waste.

It only took a few minutes to reach the bottom of the hill. As soon as I got to the bottom, I saw Josh's mom pulling into the driveway. Perfect timing. I waved, and she waved back.

Josh waved too and then he rode his bike past me. "See you tomorrow," he said.

Well, that was that.

Chapter 6

Your Secret's Safe With Me

The next morning, Josh's mom came down the hill to pick me up. I was waiting by the mailbox like I always did.

"Good morning, Andy," said Josh's mom as I opened the car door.

"Good morning," I replied.

"Hey, Andy," said Josh. He had his backpack on the seat next to him, and he was carrying a plastic bag.

Then it hit me. The snake! He really was going to bring that snake to school.

Josh had done some crazy things before, but this was the craziest. He had joked about it yesterday, but a real snake wasn't a joke.

Josh's mom didn't like animals. And she definitely didn't like snakes. She'd freak if she knew there was one in her car!

If I said anything that tipped her off, we would both be in big trouble. It wasn't my snake, so I didn't want to get in trouble for it. No way!

"Hey," I said back. I looked over at Josh's mom. I didn't say a word. I didn't want to give it away. But I gave Josh a look.

Josh looked at me like nothing was going on. He acted like it was just any other day. But he was going to have one of those wild and crazy days, and things were going to end badly. I just knew it.

Maybe I could convince Josh to stop this crazy plan before he went too far. Sometimes I could talk Josh out of his "great" ideas.

And other days, nothing I said made any difference to Josh. He didn't listen to me. He just did whatever he wanted.

So what kind of day was it going to be?

We went down the hill and turned right at the first stop sign. Then we drove to the end of the street and turned left. The bus stop was right there.

The bus was already there waiting for us. We were the first stop, so sometimes Henry showed up early to drink his coffee. He said he liked to soak in the peace and quiet before us crazy kids kept him on his toes for the rest of the day. He was standing over by the creek holding his cup of coffee.

Josh's mom pulled up behind the bus. "Thanks, Ms. Jamison," I said, and then I opened the door and hopped out. I wanted to get out of there as fast as I could!

Josh, on the other hand, was taking his sweet time getting out of the car.

Hurry, before your mom discovers there's a snake in her car!

"Bye, Mom," Josh said, and then he opened the door and got out of the car with the bag in one hand and his backpack in the other.

Josh's mom waved good-bye as she drove away.

Well, Josh dodged a bullet there. But I had to know, when was he going to let the snake out of the bag? If he did that on the bus, Henry would just pull over, let us off at the curb, and drive away. At least, that's what he threatened to do last year when Caleb tried to bring those firecrackers on the bus.

The school didn't let Caleb ride the bus for the rest of year. Snakes weren't against the law like firecrackers were, but Henry didn't like it when people didn't follow the rules. And I'm pretty sure that letting a snake loose on the bus broke some sort of rule.

Maybe I could talk Josh into letting the snake go now. There were lots of bushes by the bus stop. The snake could go down by the creek and live there. It was better for the snake, and it was better for Josh, too. But would he do that?

I walked over to Josh. "Why did you bring the snake?" I whispered.

"I told you I was going to bring it to school," said Josh. "My mom didn't suspect a thing!"

What about Henry? How could Josh get the snake on the bus without him finding out?

I had to do something, or this was going to be a disaster! I just knew it.

"Why don't you let the snake out down here at the bus stop? It can live over there by the creek, and you won't get in trouble."

"I'm not going to let my snake go now," said Josh. "I told you I was going to bring it to school to scare Megan, and I will."

"But not on the bus," I said. "Remember what almost happened to Caleb last year."

Josh shook his head. "You worry too much."

I knew better than to say any more. When Josh got something on his mind, he just didn't budge. He wasn't going to change his mind no matter what I said.

I looked over at Henry. He was drinking his coffee as if nothing was wrong. Well, it wasn't yet, and I wasn't going to tattle. "Better get on the bus quickly before Henry comes over."

"That was the plan," said Josh, and he sauntered over and climbed up the steps.

I followed Josh onto the bus. Emma was sitting in the front like always. She gave Josh a strange look when she saw him holding the plastic bag, but she didn't say anything, so I didn't say anything either.

We headed for our usual row. Josh walked past the other kids on the bus and put the plastic bag down on the backseat. Then he put his backpack next to him.

"Are you crazy?" I said.

"Shush, you'll give it away," said Josh.

"But what if . . . ," I said, and then I stopped.

"If it gets out," said Josh as he touched the slider on the backpack's zipper.

Was he going to let the snake out on the bus? "Don't do that!" I said.

Josh took his hand off the zipper and laughed. Then I heard boots. Henry was on the bus! I turned to see if he was coming this way, but Henry didn't suspect a thing. He stood at the front of the bus and counted, "One, two, three, four, five, six, seven, eight, nine. Everyone is here, so let's go."

Henry sat down, put on his seat belt, and started up the bus. He pulled the metal lever, and the bus door closed. I moved across the backseat to the window on the other side. I didn't want to sit by the snake. No way! But there was no going back now. Josh was bringing a snake to school. I had a very bad feeling about this!

At each and every stop, more kids got on the bus and sat down. But not one of them noticed that Josh had a bag *and* a backpack. As far as anyone knew it was just another Thursday morning, two days to the weekend.

When we got to school, Josh was the last one to get off the bus. He carried the bag in his arms and wore his backpack. The snake was in his backpack, but he just walked into school like there was nothing wrong. What could I do now?

I followed Josh down the hallway to the fifth grade coat hooks. I had to go there anyway.

Bam! Josh dropped the plastic bag filled with books on the floor. A few kids turned around to see what was up. Megan and her friends giggled.

If you only knew, I thought, but they didn't.

Josh put his backpack on the coat hook and unzipped it. Then he took out the paper bag with the snake inside and put it on the floor. The paper bag was folded at the top just like an ordinary bag, but that wasn't a lunch I wanted to eat. No thanks! Then he leaned down and started taking his books out of the plastic bag.

I went across the hall to my coat hook and took out my lunch. I had a baloney sandwich in there, not a snake. After I took everything else out of my backpack, I put my lunch back inside the backpack and zipped it up.

Ring!

"Let's go!" I said, and I ran down the hallway to class. I opened the front door to Ms. Clary's class and walked inside. I quickly slipped into my seat. *Phew!* I had made it before the tardy bell rang.

But where was Josh? He should have been right behind me. I turned and looked back at his desk by the window, but Josh wasn't sitting there yet. So where was he?

Ring!

There was the tardy bell. Just then, I heard a scream from the hallway.

"Ahhh! Snake!"

I quickly turned to see if Megan was at her desk, but she wasn't. Megan and Josh were still in the hallway. And from the sound of it, the snake was out of the bag.

The Ending Is Up2U!

If you want Andy to go out into the hallway and help his friend, go to page 51.

→ OR ←

If you want Andy to act like he doesn't know anything, go to page 63.

→ OR ←

If you want Andy to ask the science teacher for help, go to page 71.

ENDING
→ 1 ←

Out of the Bag

I stood up and ran to the door at the back of the classroom. I opened and closed the door quietly so Ms. Clary wouldn't hear me leave. She was writing something on the board so she didn't see me. Maybe I could fix this before she knew I was gone.

I looked down the hallway and saw Megan's backpack lying open on the ground. But Megan was nowhere to be seen, and Josh . . . Where was Josh?

I turned and looked down the hallway the other way. Josh was on his knees under the backpacks by the front door of Ms. Clary's class. Some kids had left their lunches and their PE shoes on the floor, so Josh was slowly lifting them up one by one.

"Where's the snake?" I asked as I ran over to Josh, but he didn't even look at me. He just kept lifting things up one by one.

Before I could say another word, the classroom door opened in front of us and Ms. Clary came out. "What are you two doing out here in the hallway? Come in the room, please. Class has started."

So much for getting this fixed before she noticed I was gone. The snake was out of the bag now, but where was it? I needed time to help Josh find it, so I told Ms. Clary the truth. "We're looking for Josh's snake," I said.

Then I saw something blue. The snake must have been hiding under the classroom door. But now it was slithering into our classroom. I had to do something fast! "Don't move!" I said.

Ms. Clary took a deep breath and then she started yelling at us. "Just who do you think you are? You and your friend are in a boatload of trouble."

Well, that shook Josh up. He finally stopped lifting lunches and shoes and looked up. Now he could see where his little blue snake had gone. It was right next to the teacher's shoe!

Josh jumped up and ran toward Ms. Clary.

"My snake! Don't step on my snake!"

At last, Ms. Clary looked down and saw the snake. She jumped back in surprise. At the same time, our classmates started screaming. Ms. Clary tried to calm them, but the screaming didn't stop. It only got louder.

Some kids jumped up on the desks. Others just lifted their feet up off the ground.

Everyone in the class was afraid of the snake. Well, everyone except Emma. She walked right up to Josh.

"So that was why you had a bag *and* a backpack on the bus this morning, wasn't it?" demanded Emma.

But Josh just waved her off.

Josh thought he could fake out Emma, but he forgot she was Caleb's little sister. Caleb had gotten into way more trouble than Josh ever had.

"What are you going to do about this, Josh?" said Emma, as she leaned in and stared him down.

"Not now, Emma," said Josh.

But Emma was having none of that. She just followed him and kept talking. "That little blue snake didn't ask to come here, Josh. You brought it here, so you better keep it safe."

And then the snake moved toward them, making them both jump back. Then it slithered over to the first row of desks and disappeared.

"The snake went under those desks!" yelled Josh. "Help me move them out of the way."

Madison and Hannah jumped off their desks and ran to the back of the classroom and climbed up on some empty desks.

"This is all your fault, Josh!" screamed Madison. "Why did you have to bring a snake to school anyway?"

Josh pushed the two empty desks aside, but they fell over, so Josh started screaming too.

"No, no, no, no! Don't fall on my snake!"

"Get that snake away from me," yelled Christopher as he ran to the back of the classroom.

Other kids followed him, but there weren't any more empty desks, so they crawled up on the shelves by the window.

Hannah opened the window and starting yelling, "Snake! It's a snake! Get me out of here!"

Josh lifted up the first desk, but the little blue snake wasn't there.

I lifted the second desk, but the snake wasn't under that one either. *Where was it?*

"Move those desks out of the way so we can find it," said Josh, pointing to the next row.

"And what exactly are you looking for, Mr. Jamison?" said a deep voice from the hallway. Mr. Franks was standing in the open door,

and Emma was standing right behind him. She must have gone to his class to ask for help.

There was nothing I could say that would make it better, so I let Josh do the talking. "It's my snake . . . my blue garter snake. It got out of the bag . . . and it's just a baby . . . Please don't hurt it."

"All of you are much bigger than a baby snake, so you don't have anything to fear," said Mr. Franks. "It's much more scared of you than you are of it.

"Fear of snakes is quite common," said Mr. Franks as he walked into the classroom. "In fact, fear of snakes is the most common fear people have. But you all knew Cornflower, and he never hurt you, did he?"

All around me, kids shook their heads. No, Cornflower had never hurt anyone.

Mr. Franks walked over and stood next to Ms. Clary. "Now let's take these students next door to my classroom so we can look for this little baby."

Ms. Clary spoke to the class. "I want everyone to line up at the back door and follow me into the science room."

"But what about my pencil case?" said Madison, worried to leave anything behind with the snake still on the loose.

"Leave all your things right where they are," said Mr. Franks. "You can come back for them in a few minutes." Then he looked over at us. "I want you two to stay right where you are until I get back. You caused this mess, so you're going to clean it up."

All of the other students lined up behind Ms. Clary and Mr. Franks. In less than a minute the room was empty.

We were going to be in a lot of trouble. *A lot* of trouble!

I turned and looked at Josh, but he was on the floor under Ms. Clary's desk. The little blue snake must have slithered over there. How were we ever going to catch it now? I wasn't going to put my hand under the teacher's desk to grab a snake.

Ms. Clary had a long wooden pointer with a black rubber tip at the end. I ran over to the board and picked it up.

I kneeled on the floor behind Ms. Clary's desk and looked underneath. The little blue snake was coiled up by one of the legs. I moved the pointer over and tried to pull it out from under the desk.

"Be careful. Don't hurt it," said Josh.

Then I heard footsteps. "Didn't I tell you two to clean up this mess?" asked Mr. Franks.

Josh stood up and started talking. "But this is how we caught it the last time—with a long stick and a bag."

"I didn't ask you to catch the snake," said Mr. Franks. "I asked you to clean up the mess you made." He waved a gloved hand at the overturned desks. "I know how to handle a snake."

I came out from behind Ms. Clary's desk.

Mr. Franks was wearing the long gloves he used when he cleaned the snake tank.

"But . . . but . . . Mr. Franks," stammered Josh.

"You must really like detention, Mr. Jamison," said Mr. Franks. "You already had one week, but now I think two is best. Yes, two weeks for both of you. Unless you'd like more?"

No! Two weeks of detention meant two weeks of no bike rides!

I walked over and put the pointer stick back. How did I get into these messes? Whenever I tried to help Josh, I always got into trouble, too.

But I didn't want *three* weeks of detention, so I started cleaning up. I picked up all the desks in the second row, while Mr. Franks caught the snake.

The door opened, and Principal Clements came in with Megan. Her face was all red, like she'd been crying. Megan took a deep breath and pointed her finger at Josh.

"He put a snake in my backpack!" she said, and then she started crying again.

"And what do you have to say for yourself, Mr. Jamison?" asked Ms. Clements. "Is that how we expect students to act at this school?"

Well, what could Josh say? He brought the snake to school and it had turned into a disaster, just like I knew it would.

Josh looked down at the floor and didn't say a word.

And what about you, Mr. Johnson? You seem to have a hand in this little plan."

I hung my head and mumbled, "I'm sorry."

"I've given the boys two weeks of detention for this mess," said Mr. Franks. "But now . . ."

"But now I think we need to get their parents involved," said Ms. Clements.

No, no, no! Now I would be grounded for weeks!

"I want you both to come to my office after you are done here," said Ms. Clements. Then she looked at Megan. "Come with me, dear," she said softly. "Let's go get your backpack."

"Okay," sniffed Megan, and she left with Ms. Clements.

"Put everything back the way it was," said Mr. Franks, and then he walked out the door with the snake.

I wished I could put that snake back in the nest and just leave it up there in the hills. But it was too late for that now.

Ending
→ 2 ←
Stop and Breathe

I heard laughter coming from the hallway. I knew that laugh. It was Josh laughing at Megan just like he said he would. There was no way she was going to keep this a secret. Now Megan would tell on him, and he would be in big trouble.

I knew bringing the snake to school was going to be a disaster. Josh was my best friend, but I couldn't remember the last time one of his great ideas actually worked. He had lived across the street from me all my life. He was a good friend. But when his great ideas got him into trouble, they got me into trouble, too.

"No, no, no," said a voice in the hallway.

Now what?

"My snake!" cried Josh, and then I knew the snake was loose and things had gone from bad to worse.

I turned and looked at the clock. School had started less than a minute ago, and Josh was out in the hallway with Megan and a snake. A snake that was loose. Who knew where it would go.

So what was I going to do now? I closed my eyes and took a deep breath. I could hear loud voices and bumping sounds in the hall, but I ignored them.

The snake wasn't my problem right now. I didn't bring the snake to school. Josh did. I had tried to talk him out of it, knowing it would get him in trouble. I was keeping myself out of trouble this time.

I opened my eyes and looked at the small window in the classroom door. I saw Principal Clements walk by, but that wasn't a surprise.

Once again, Josh's great ideas were going to land him in the principal's office.

A few minutes later, the door opened and the principal came in with Josh and Megan. "Please excuse the interruption, Ms. Clary," said Ms. Clements. "Megan has been helping me in the office, so please mark her as present, not tardy."

"Of course, Ms. Clements," said Ms. Clary.

The whole class was staring at Megan and Josh. They didn't know what was going on, and I wasn't going to say a thing. I was going to stay out of trouble this time.

Megan's eyes were red, like she had been crying. But no one said anything about it while Ms. Clements was standing there.

"Mister Jamison here will be going home," said Ms. Clements.

Why did he have to go home? Why wasn't he going to get detention like he always did? Something strange was going on.

"Please mark Joshua absent for today, Ms. Clary," said Ms. Clements.

"Yes, Ms. Clements," said Ms. Clary.

Josh just stood there next to Ms. Clements. He didn't look at me. He didn't look at anyone.

"Thank you, Ms. Clary," said the principal, and then she walked out of the classroom. Josh followed her without saying a word.

"What's going on?" asked Emma.

Ms. Clary shook her head. "It's none of our business. Now, open your books to page 43."

English class went on without Josh. It was as if he had never been there that day at all. Josh and the snake were just forgotten.

I was working on page 44 when I heard a noise outside the window. It was Josh and his mom. She was talking in a very loud voice.

"I cannot believe you did this to me and today of all days when I had that big client coming to town for a meeting. Do you know how embarrassing this is? To be called to the principal's office in the middle of an important meeting because your only child is suspended!"

I could hardly believe my ears. Suspended! Josh was suspended from school? That was even worse than detention.

"But Mom, I was only . . . ," said Josh as he started to explain.

That only made his mom angrier!

"No, don't say another word! I don't want to hear your excuses. Now go get in the car so I can go back to work. What am I going to do with you? You're in fifth grade now. You should know better than to bring a snake to school. Now I have to pay for child care—for a ten-year-old! I hope you have fun spending the next week in the infant care center at work."

Josh turned and looked at his mom but she raised her hand. "Not a word. Just go and get in the car."

English class ended a few minutes later, so I went to math without Josh. It felt strange. I had gone to school for a day or two before without Josh. But a whole *week?* Josh had never been out of school that long. A week without seeing Josh was going to be weird, and who knew how long he would be grounded after that.

I sat with Ethan and Matt at lunch, just like Josh and I always did. Then we went to music and PE and then it was time for the last class of the day, science. The whole school day went by, just like it always did, but Josh wasn't there.

I walked into the science room and then I saw it. The little blue snake was in the terrarium at the back of the class. Mr. Franks's snake, Cornflower, had lived in that tank, well, as long as I had been at this school, but he had died at the beginning of the school year. And now, there was the baby snake Josh and I had caught, right there in the tank.

So Josh's great idea had worked out after all. It hadn't worked out so well for Josh. I mean, he was suspended from school for a week. But for the snake and for Mr. Franks, it was going to be okay.

I walked over to the terrarium and bent down so I could look that snake right in the eyes. Did it recognize me? Ha! Even if it did, that snake wasn't talking. I was not in trouble this time because I had stayed out of Josh's crazy plan. I stopped and took a breath. I can't make Josh do the right thing, but I can choose to do the right thing for myself.

Ending

3

Ask for Help

A snake in the hallway? Uh-oh.

I raised my hand. "Ms. Clary, Ms. Clary," I said.

"Yes, what is it, Andy?" said Ms. Clary.

"Mr. Franks used to have a snake," I said. "He'll know what to do." I waited for Ms. Clary to answer.

"Yes, Mr. Franks did have a snake and he named it Cornflower," said Emma. "But the snake was brown, white, and orange, so the name didn't match." The girls sitting around her all giggled.

Why do girls always have to laugh at everything?

Then I noticed Emma wasn't laughing. She turned and gave me a look. That's when I knew Emma had figured it out.

Well, she did see Josh get on the bus with a bag and a backpack, and her brother *was* Caleb. Caleb had gotten into more trouble than Josh ever did. And Josh was in trouble a lot, so that was saying something.

"It was a corn snake, so that's why he named it that," I said.

"Well, he did have that strange blue flower in the terrarium. But why was it in there? Couldn't it hurt the snake?" said Emma.

The girls giggled again.

"It was just a plastic flower. It didn't hurt anything," I said.

Emma shook her head. "Why would anyone want a plastic flower? Plastic hurts the environment. It takes hundreds of millions of years to break down. When I . . ."

"Thank you, Emma," interrupted Ms. Clary finally.

"Yes, Andy, you can go talk to Mr. Franks," said Ms. Clary.

Emma gave me another look, and then I realized she had been stalling the teacher. Was she trying to help Josh, or hurt him? I wasn't sure.

"Thanks, Ms. Clary," I said, and then I ran to the door. Mr. Franks was already in the hallway. But where was Josh? Had he been sent to the principal's office?

I walked over to Mr. Franks. He was wearing his long snake-handling gloves as he crouched by the backpacks that had been knocked to the floor.

"Excuse me, Mr. Franks," I said.

"Can it wait? I'm kind of busy now, Andy," said Mr. Franks. "There's a snake on the loose." He seemed very disturbed.

"I can help you with that," I said.

Mr. Franks stopped looking at the backpacks on the floor. "You can help? I'm all ears."

"When Josh and I . . . ," I said, and then I stopped. Oh no, I'd just given it away. Now Josh was going to be in trouble for sure, well, if he wasn't already in trouble by now.

"Go on," said Mr. Franks in a patient voice.

"Well, when we saw the nest of baby snakes, there were so many of them and they were all crawling all over each other. Josh wanted to bring one to school to show everyone, but I didn't want to put my hand in their nest."

"No, that's not a good idea," said Mr. Franks, and he lifted both hands. His gloves almost reached his elbows. "I always wear these gloves when I handle a snake. Reptiles have salmonella in their gastrointestinal tract. The salmonella doesn't hurt the snake, but it's harmful to humans and can make you feel quite sick. Some people even have to be hospitalized."

"You can get that sick from just touching it?" I said as I looked at my hands.

"Did you touch the snake?" asked Mr. Franks.

"No, I only lifted the snake with a stick," I said. "That's how we, well, how Josh caught it."

"Using a stick to handle a snake is actually a common practice," said Mr. Franks. "We'll borrow one from the janitor's closet. A broom or a mop with a long handle will serve our purpose."

I followed Mr. Franks down the fifth grade hallway. Mr. Manny, the school janitor, kept all of his supplies in a closet there. Mr. Franks opened the janitor's closet door and we walked inside. The cleaning cart was gone, but there was an old mop leaning against the wall.

"Look what we have here," said Mr. Franks. "I didn't think it had come this far."

And then I saw it. The little blue snake was in the old mop! It was crawling in the long white strings of the mop. It must have thought the strings were other snakes!

Mr. Franks reached over and grabbed the long wooden handle of the mop. "Can you hold the handle while I get the snake untangled?"

"Sure," I said, reaching out my hand to hold the mop steady.

Mr. Franks leaned down and took the little blue snake out of the mop strings. "That's no home for a pretty little snake like you." He held the snake in his gloved hand like he wasn't afraid of it at all.

"Let's take you to a safer place," Mr. Franks said to the snake as he walked down the hallway.

The little snake tried to crawl off the glove, but Mr. Franks didn't look worried. He just moved his other hand up so the snake crawled on that glove instead. Mr. Franks smiled as the little snake crawled across his gloves.

I ran over and opened the door to the science room. The whole class started talking when we walked into the room.

"Can I see it?" asked Tamika.

"Don't bring it over here!" said Jamal. "I hate snakes!"

Mr. Franks walked over to the terrarium on the shelf at the back of the class. It had been Cornflower's home for many years, but now it was just sitting there, empty.

"Andy, can you open the terrarium, please?" asked Mr. Franks.

I ran over to the shelf and lifted up the heavy wooden top.

"Thank you," said Mr. Franks, and he leaned over and put both gloves into the terrarium. The little blue snake climbed onto the thick branch inside it. After the snake climbed off his gloves, Mr. Franks pulled down the top and locked it.

Mr. Franks looked over at me. "What shall we name it?"

Name it? Did that mean he was going to keep it? I guess it did. I looked at the little blue snake as it crawled around its new home. Cornflower's blue plastic flower was still there in the corner, sticking out of the gravel.

"Little Blue," I said.

"Perfect," said Mr. Franks. "Just perfect."

And it was. Mr. Franks had a new snake, and I was not in trouble. A disaster had turned into a win. And it was only first period.

"Andy, please go to the principal's office and tell Ms. Clements we have the snake in the terrarium," said Mr. Franks. "Ask her to send Megan here so I can show her the snake won't hurt her. And ask Ms. Clements to send Josh here, too. I have to talk to Josh about the proper way to treat a snake. Live animals are not toys."

Mr. Franks smiled. "And in last period, you and Josh can both tell the class where and how you found the snake."

"Yes, Mr. Franks," I said, and then I went to get Josh and Megan. Josh probably had detention, but I didn't, and now the little blue snake had a good home. It was going to be a pretty good day after all.

Write Your Own Ending

There were three endings to choose from in *A Great Idea?* Did you find the ending you wanted from the story, or did you want something different to happen? Now it is your turn! Write the ending you would like to see. Be creative!